For Rana Esculenta

and with thanks to my two guinea pigs
Rose and Albert

Copyright © 2008 by William Bee

First U.S. edition 2008

Library of Congress Cataloging-in-Publication Data is available.
Library of Congress Catalog Card Number 2007040401

ISBN 978-0-7636-3920-4

10 9 8 7 6 5 4 3
Printed in China
This book was typeset in Plantin and Rockwell.
The illustrations were done in pen, ink and Macintosh.

Candlewick Press
2067 Massachusetts Avenue
Cambridge, Massachusetts 02140
visit us at www.candlewick.com

BEWARE OF THE FROG

william bee

CANDLEWICK PRESS

This is the story
of a sweet little old lady
named Mrs. Collywobbles.

Mrs. Collywobbles lives in
a little house on the edge of
a big, dark, scary wood.

The only thing protecting
Mrs. Collywobbles from all
the horrible creatures that live
in the big, dark, scary wood is . . .

her little pet frog.

Look! There is little Mrs. Collywobbles,
hiding in her kitchen.
Who has she seen coming
out of the big, dark, scary wood?

Oh, dear!
It's that terrible thief,
Greedy Goblin, up to
no good, out stealing from
sweet little old ladies.

"*Nickerty-noo, nickerty-noo,*
if I get a chance,
I'll steal from you. . . .

I love to steal money
and shiny, pretty things. . . .
I'm in and out of the house
in a flash."

"What's this? **BEWARE OF THE FROG**?
Well, no frog will keep me from getting what
I want. Maybe I'll just steal that frog, too!

Nickerty-noo, nickerty-noo,
if I get a chance,
I'll steal from you. . . ."

And so Greedy Goblin quietly
opens the gate.

But oh, dear, the frog doesn't
look very pleased about that. . . .

Look! There is little Mrs. Collywobbles,
hiding in her bathroom.
Who has she seen coming
out of the big, dark, scary wood?

Oh, dear!

It's Smelly Troll, up to no good.
He moves into little old ladies'
houses and stinks so much that
they have to run away.

"*Welly-welly, welly-welly,*
I'm awfully slimy
and awfully smelly. . . .

This little old lady's house is
just what I've been looking for. . . .
I'll whiff something rotten,
so she'll soon run away."

"What's this? **BEWARE OF THE FROG**?
I'll belch and reek and stink so much,
that frog will have to hop off, too!

Welly-welly, welly-welly,
I'm awfully slimy
and awfully smelly. . . ."

And so, with a whiff,
Smelly Troll opens the gate.

But oh, dear, the frog doesn't
look very pleased about that. . . .

BEWARE OF THE FROG

Look! There is little Mrs. Collywobbles,
hiding in her bedroom.
Who has she seen coming
out of the big, dark, scary wood?

Oh, dear! Oh, dear!

It's Giant Hungry Ogre!

He wants his supper,

and his favorite food is . . .

sweet little old lady.

"*Dum-de-dum, dum-de-dummy,*
I've got a very, very hungry tummy. . . .

This looks promising. . . .

My belly's rumbling, and

I must have my supper—

a juicy old lady

cooked in lots of

honey and butter."

"What's this? **BEWARE OF THE FROG**?
Yum-yum, that frog will taste lovely
dipped in some ketchup.

Dum-de-dum, dum-de-dummy,
I've got a very, very hungry tummy. . . ."

And so Giant Hungry Ogre
licks his lips and opens the gate.

But oh, dear, the frog doesn't
look very pleased about that. . . .

So that was the story of a sweet
little old lady named Mrs. Collywobbles,
who lived next to a big, dark, scary wood.

And as you can see, Mrs. Collywobbles
no longer has to spend all her time hiding
in her little house. And it's all thanks to . . .

her little pet frog.

"Oh, my little froggy friend,
how can I ever thank you?"
asks Mrs. Collywobbles.

The frog thinks for a moment. . . .

"How about a little kiss?"
suggests the frog.
So Mrs. Collywobbles
gives him a little kiss . . . and . . .

HEY PRESTO!

Mrs. Collywobbles is transformed

into a sweet little old lady . . . frog.

But oh, dear, she doesn't look

very pleased about that . . .

does she?

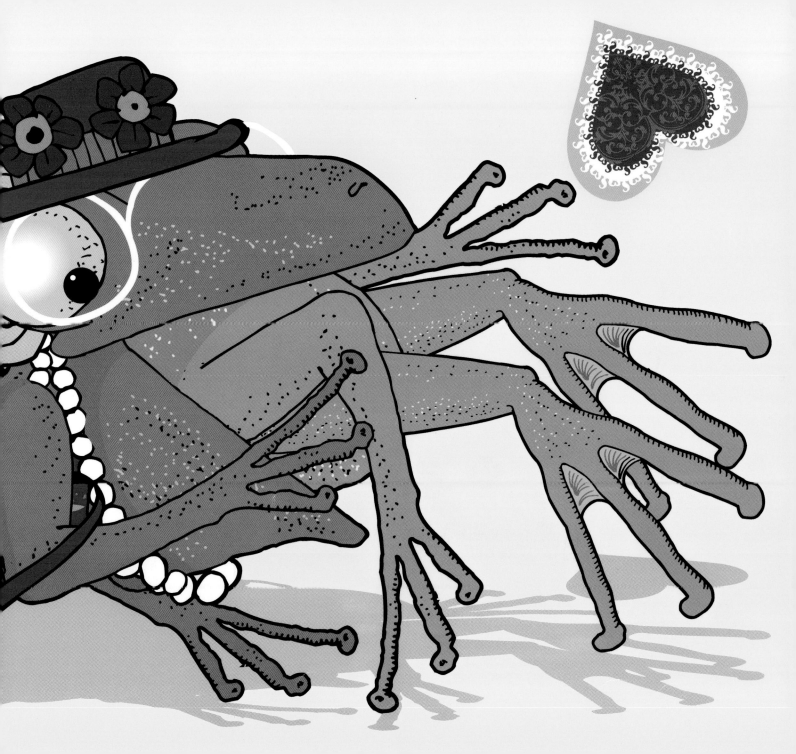